LAGOON

THALIA S. A.

MERMAID
LAGOON

Illustrated by Ann J. & Thalia S.A.

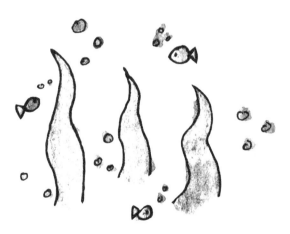

I would dedicate my book to Mum, Dad, and my brother Zayd. Though I will not do that.

So instead I am dedicating it to...

My brother Zayd, Dad, and Mum.

Because Zayd doesn't want to be put last just because he's the youngest.

Moreover, thank you to: Mrs Parkinson, Miss Evans, Mrs Khaira, Miss List, Mrs Lambert and Miss Younghusband for your effort in teaching me English at school.

Contents

Mermaids have been on this planet the WHOLE time. No humans, not even a single one of them has ever discovered them. Mermaid Lagoon lies just beneath the seabeds, the place where all mermaids live.

Very few humans have ever seen a mermaid. If they have been fortunate to have, no-one believes them. Would you believe your friend if they claimed to have seen one? Most likely not.

Mermaid Lagoon is a place full of wonder, mystery and secrets. A place where the most magical things can happen. But there *is* a way to enter. A simple way that only allows those pure of true hearts. A simple way that requires only four words. A simple way that even a baby could try.

The unbreakable!

The indestructible!

The... "I AM A MERMAID!"

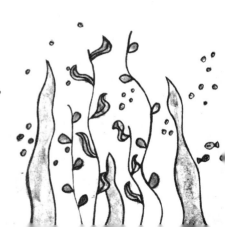

7

Chapter One

Ocean Academy

Lilly woke to the smell of the colourful flowers that sat on her windowsill. She yawned sleepily and folded back her pink polka-dot duvet. She was a ten year old girl with blonde hair and a friendly smile.

Although she was nice, Lilly would always shrink back shyly whenever strangers wanted to talk to her. Despite this, she could be determined at desperate times, especially when she needed to be.

Lilly was about to grab one of her favourite books that she liked to read, when she heard someone calling out to her.

"LILLY!" called someone.

"What do you want, Mum?" asked Lilly, responding to the voice that was clearly her mum.

"Just come to the kitchen!"

"OK, wait!"

"No waiting!"

"Fine... coming!"

Lilly plodded downstairs, still tired from her sleep. Soon enough, after what seemed like ages, she had finally reached the kitchen.

"Yes?" said Lilly, yawning. "I thought you were calling me."

"I was," said Mum. "To show you this."

Mum handed Lilly a small leaflet. On it, were pictures of a sea with details about a school.

"Why is this about a school?" questioned Lilly.

Have you ever heard the words 'sea' and 'school' in the same sentence? I didn't think so.

"Read it," urged Mum.

It read,

School on the sea! It's called Ocean Academy.
For children between ages of 8 to 11.
This amazing school is built on wooden
platforms, and is a great sight.

There'll be normal subjects, but also
other special skills, including
surfing, cooking and lots more.

It's also an amazing society of
people who want to
save the oceans!

The first term will be FREE!
To join, contact us at
Ocean Academy.

Ocean Academy

"Wow!" breathed Lilly.

"Wow indeed! Would you like to go? It is free, after all," explained her mother.

"That would be nice. But how would I get there each morning?"

"Don't be silly, it's a boarding school!"

"Wait, what?"

"Yes! I'll give you today to decide. Tell me if you'd like to go tomorrow, after you have given it some thought."

Lilly felt terribly sick. The answer was of course, no! She always felt nervous when friends came around, or when she had to perform on stage. She would have to share a dorm with some other girls if she chose to attend the school, but the school was on the sea. Lilly loved the sea with all her heart even though she had never even been there, and hadn't even been to the beach. However, she always thought about it. If she went there, it would be a dream come true! Despite all of this, Lilly told herself that she wouldn't go. She was too worried.

Later that night, Lilly shut the door and sat in the darkness, while everyone was asleep. She was still thinking about the opportunity to attend Ocean Academy.

Should I go or not? I love the sea, but I don't like the idea of a boarding school, she thought to herself. After a few minutes, her head was moaning with conflicting thoughts flying around in her head.

The busyness of her mind made her succumb to sleep. Not long after drifting off to sleep, Lilly started to dream. For Lilly, sleeping was a simple task. She peered over her shoulder and saw the sea! It was a breathtaking sight. She gazed happily at the lapping waves and felt the cool breeze. It made her think, *If I go to Ocean Academy, won't the sea be even more exciting than a dream?*

Without warning, the breeze turned into a strong torrent of wind and it pushed her forwards! She lost her footing and fell into the sea! All at once, she saw a flurry of light, and everything was spinning. Her head felt dizzy as she plummeted further and further, deep into the ocean.

"AAAAAAH!" screamed Lilly, shocked at how she could speak underwater. "SOMEONE HELP ME!" She desperately shouted and yelled at the top of her lungs, but no-one came. She carried on doing this until she hit the sandy seabed.

She saw strands of seaweed, lots of fish and shells scattered across the sea floor.

Trying to get up, Lilly instantly heard a mysterious voice. The voice sounded slightly eerie, but also calming and gentle.

"Lilly," called the voice. "Your destiny is at Ocean Academy."

"Huh?" said Lilly, feeling rather confused.

"I don't have much time to talk to you! You must go to Ocean Academy and find three other girls! Together, you must find the Crystal Clam!"

"What do you mean?" Lilly said, still feeling perplexed.

"Do what I say! You cannot fail or Mermaid Lagoon will be..."

Lilly opened her eyes. She blinked. It was morning.

"Come on! Why, oh why did I wake up? I need to find out more!" yelled Lilly.

Even though it was just a dream, something in her heart told her that this voice was real. She truly sensed that there was a whole mystery out there to be solved. Though if she wanted to find out, she'd have to make a brave, bold decision. She took a deep breath and walked to the kitchen, where her mum was.

Lilly sat down at the table and munched on some cereal.

"Hello Lilly!" smiled Mum. "Did you have a good sleep?"

"You could say that," mumbled Lilly.

"So what's your decision then?" asked Mum. "Do you want to go to Ocean Academy?"

This was it. This was where Lilly's path to victory was to begin.

But if she wanted destiny, she'd have to choose the correct track to success. What would her answer be?

"I'd like to go, please," she decided bravely.

"Are you sure?" queried her mum.

"I'm sure."

"OK! Remember to pack! You'll be leaving in two weeks' time."

"OK Mum. I'm going to pack now."

After their short conversation, Lilly's decision was made.

She skipped upstairs, feeling proud of herself.

I did it! Now I must look out for three girls and find something called the Crystal Clam, she thought.

Putting things into her suitcase, Lilly immediately felt a knot in her stomach.

But then she remembered her dream and what she was going to do. It was then that she felt confident.

She shouted, "I will do it, and no-one will stop me! I will go to Ocean Academy, and save the mermaids! I will-"

"Lilly?" whispered a voice.

It was Zack, her little brother. He had madly messy hair and a disgustingly dirty face. He could be annoying, but sometimes useful and fun.

18

"Yes, Zack?" Lilly answered.

"Did you know-" started Zack, but was interrupted.

"What? Another animal fact?" Lilly thought, knowing that her brother loved animals.

"Yes! Tigers' ears twist a little bit when they're angry!" proclaimed Zack.

"Wow, that's cool!" smiled Lilly.

"You also forgot your book," Zack pointed out, handing over a thick book.

"Oh, thank you," smiled Lilly, taking the book happily.

He smiled but stayed in the doorway.

"What now?" she asked.

"I want a reward," he grinned.

"OK then," Lilly chuckled.

Lilly handed him a sweet that had sat in the dark depths of her pocket. Zack beamed and stuffed it into his mouth with greed. Lilly just laughed to see him so happy.

Sometimes he was quite nice, although that was her last hidden sweet.

(She liked to stash sweets in every room. They were useful when she was hungry, especially if she was told to eat something like a carrot.)

Zack then left, pleased at last.

Lilly went back to thinking about her peculiar dream. Who was that voice, and what did it mean? After a while, she became easily distracted by the book Zack had given her.

"Oooh," said Lilly, as she flipped the pages.

It was a story all about some sailors. She came to a part where they got sucked into a whirlpool.

For those who have no clue about what a whirlpool is, it's a strong body of water swirled round and round. She read on for a few minutes, enjoying the story. All of a sudden, a small parcel fell out of the book.

She observed it closely and the parcel was not wrapped with paper, but with seaweed! The seaweed smelt faintly of the beach, and that started to make her excited.

"Wow!" she exclaimed, eyes wide. "Who put this in here?"

Lilly at once knew it couldn't have been anyone in her family that placed the small parcel there, because they had never been to the sea or beach. But then who had left the parcel there? Hmm, Zack did pass her the book. Could he have tampered with her book? Surely not. He was not interested in books at all, unless it was about an animal. Where would he have even found the parcel?

She slowly unwrapped it, not wanting to break what was inside. At last she saw a golden gleam pouring out from the parcel. It was a pearl!

The shiny pearl was golden and it sounded like waves of the ocean when she put it to her ear.

21

It was reflective, so she could see her face in it. She slipped the pearl into her pocket, not wanting to lose it.

Lilly closed her suitcase in both fear and excitement. She was going to go to Ocean Academy, and nothing was going to stop her!

Chapter Two

Follow that girl (or spy on her)

When two weeks had passed, Lilly was woken up by her dad. She pulled herself out of bed and yawned loudly.

"Huh? It's not morning yet," said Lilly, staring out the window. It seemed dark, and there were still a few stars sprinkled in the sky.

"No Lilly, it's morning! It's just very early," laughed Dad, seeing his daughter's confused face.

Lilly grabbed her suitcase and the pair stumbled to the bus stop.

She looked around at the dew that was delicately resting on the plants and she felt the cold air on her cheeks. It felt strange to be leaving all this so soon.

23

"Isn't the bus meant to be coming now?" asked Lilly.

"It is. It's probably late or something," her dad remarked.

A few minutes later, the bus had arrived. She hauled herself up and pulled her luggage up behind her. She yanked her head out the window as far as she could, though it made her look ridiculous.

"Bye Dad!" Lilly called, almost falling out the window.

"Bye Lilly!" called her dad, waving as the bus started to drive away.

Lilly waved and waved until her father was nothing but a speck in the distance.

She fingered the golden pearl in her pocket. She knew that she had to carry it with her whilst on her journey. Lilly told herself, *turning back is NOT an option. I MUST go to Ocean Academy.*

Throughout the journey, the bus would sometimes stop to pick up passengers, and one of them sat next to Lilly.

She had a cheeky but friendly face, with brown hair tied in two ponytails. She seemed to be daring and confident. Lilly peered at her warily, feeling shy.

"Hi, I'm Mia," said the girl.

Lilly felt scared but she wanted to be friends. After all, she would be lonely if no-one was there for her.

"Oh, hello Mia. I'm Lilly," she introduced herself.

"I'm excited to go to Ocean Academy! I've heard that there will be lots of sea animals."

"Oooh! I love sea animals!"

"That's good. Can we be friends?"

"Yes, please."

"That's settled then! What do you like to do?"

"I like to read and write. I want to be an author when I'm an adult. You?"

"I like to spy! I want to be a spy when I grow up. I sometimes play a prank or two as well! You know the biscuits called Oreos?"

"Yes?"

"Well, once I took out the cream of an Oreo and replaced it with toothpaste. Then I gave it to my older sister!"

"You must have gotten into trouble!"

"Yeah, but I didn't really mind. It was funny to see her reaction. You should try it sometime."

"Maybe not!"

"It's pretty early, so I'm gonna have a rest. Anyways, our flight is at 7 o'clock. Goodnight!"

"Goodnight!"

Lilly beamed with joy. She wasn't even at the school and she had already made a friend! A naughty one, though.

She stared at the misty clouds in the sky and smiled. Lilly suddenly realized something: *Could this be one of the four girls I need to find?*

The answer sounded like a yes. *This is easy,* she thought.

"Huh?" said Lilly, suddenly in another place. "Oh, this is a dream."

Lilly studied the place she was in, and recognized it easily. It was the same place as her previous dream, except this time, she saw a glowing, shiny clam. It sat peacefully on a bed of colourful sponge.

She remembered something: *The Crystal Clam!*

Lilly then saw a *mermaid!*

The mermaid had golden long hair to her waist, a silver crown upon her head, and an orange-coloured tail.

"The Shadow Realm are coming to attack," worried the mermaid. She sounded like the voice Lilly had previously heard!

Lilly then noticed floating black spirits flying towards some other mermaids! These spirits were mermaid-shaped, but they were made of dark mist and shadows. They had red-glowing eyes that made them look nasty, and they held weapons made out of either clouds or fog.

"WAR!!!" shouted everyone around Lilly. She herself could only just watch in amazement.

Lilly cried out as the mermaids were hurt or were being defeated by the strange spirits. This reminded her of the time when she had accidentally seen a movie about a scary war on the TV. It had given her nightmares for ages.

Meanwhile, the mermaid with the orange tail swam above, holding the Crystal Clam! Lilly watched in fear as she saw another black spirit float towards her.

The spirit had a sword, which she used to try to destroy the clam! The clam would not break, but it flew out of sight! A golden pearl flew out of it too! A darkness speedily spilled across the sea. It was as if someone had poured some dark water into the ocean. The evil spirits then took the mermaids as either servants or prisoners.

The orange-tailed mermaid quickly chanted a spell,

"I bring the Crystal Clam
To Ocean Academy.
Four girls will retrieve the clam
And bring it back to me!"

I must be one of those girls, thought Lilly. It was obvious! She had to find the clam with some other girls, then bring it back!

Lilly blinked. There was a sparkling ray of sunlight upon her face. It wasn't dark anymore. *Why am I always waking up? I want to find out more,* she thought. Although she had woken up, she now knew what the Crystal Clam looked like and what she had to do.

"Phew!" sighed Mia, waking up. "I had a scary dream."

"What was your dream about?" asked Lilly.

"Well, I saw this mermaid with an orange tail, lots of evil spirits, and a war! And then-"

"Wait a minute. I had the same dream!" Lilly said.

"Really?"

"Yes! I mean it! And before I had a dream with a voice, telling me to go to Ocean Academy! That's why I came!"

"Woah, that's weird. Because, well, I had a dream just like that!"

"This must mean..."

"What?"

"We are two of the girls that need to find the Crystal Clam!"

"Wow! That is so cool! Do you think we'll go on adventures? Or have magic spells? Maybe we'll even meet mermaids!"

"Maybe yes! But for now, let's stop thinking about all the good points of being magical. We could fail!"

"That's because we *won't* fail! Because we'll stick together, right?"

"Right!"

But before they had time to say anything else, a huge building towered over them. It was the airport! It was cream white in colour, with glass doors.

Aeroplanes from all directions zoomed up into the sapphire-blue sky. All of the children gasped in joy, knowing it was going to be exciting.

The two new friends walked into the airport, linking arms. It was so busy! There were people panicking, people eating, people... Well, you get what I mean.

"It's so packed!" yelled Mia, folding her arms.

"It is! But where do we go?" exclaimed Lilly, eyes wide.

They had no idea where to start! Even worse, they could miss their flight! The girls scratched their heads in confusion. What did a person have to do to get on a plane?

"Hmm, I think we should follow that girl over there," said Lilly, and she pointed to a girl behind her.

"Oooh, spying! Yes, let's spy on her!" said Mia, jumping up and down.

"No, not spy on her! We should go where she's going! She can lead us to the plane!"

"Oh! Well, I will spy anyway."

"For goodness sake, you and your spying! Let's just go!"

The girl they were following, (or spying on, according to Mia,) had black hair tied in a long plait. She wore a purple top with a picture of a cat on it. She seemed sporty and seemed to be around ten years old.

Firstly, they came to a place where you had to keep your luggage. Not knowing what to do, they just copied the actions of the black-haired girl.

The suitcases went onto a mini elevator and out of sight. They had no idea of where the luggage was going. Next, they were to be placed into large scanning objects. These interesting machines checked to see if you had anything with you.

Of course, the girls did not have anything dangerous at all, (why would they?) and naturally, they passed this phase and were ushered through. Finally, the rapid rush was over.

COSTA

THIS WAY

They could now have a rest and a drink.

So they walked over to Costa, (a popular place to drink and eat) and sat down with some hot chocolate.

"Hey, I think we should say thanks to the girl we were following. She did help us get here," said Lilly.

"You're right! Come on," said Mia.

The girl was just opposite them, also enjoying some hot chocolate. She seemed surprised to see two girls wanting to talk to her.

"Umm, yes?" the girl asked.

Chapter Three

Parachutes

Lilly felt her feet freeze right there on the spot. Again, she felt timid, but she had to at least thank the girl who led her safely the way through. After all, she and Mia wouldn't have gotten this far without this girl.

"Hello, I'm Lilly, this is Mia. We want to say thanks for helping us. You see, we weren't sure where to go, so we followed-"

"No, we spied-" interrupted Mia.

"No, not spied. We followed you to get here," explained Lilly.

"Oh! You're welcome then. Come and sit next to me. My name is Chloe," smiled the girl.

"Hi then Chloe," said Lilly. "You look as if you like sport!"

"Yep! I do! I always go on a run each morning, and I also play football," said Chloe.

"I thought football was for boys," said Mia.

"Football isn't only for boys! Who says it is? Girls can play it too," said Chloe.

"Maybe I should try football then," grinned Mia.

"Me too!" agreed Lilly.

Lilly now had a smile on her face, and a skip in her step. She sipped her drink in pleasure and sighed with happiness. But a thought struck her...

She scrutinized the clock on the wall. What had Mia said on the bus?

"Hold on! What did you say on the bus, Mia?" asked Lilly.

"Oh yes, the Oreo trick! Ha!" laughed Mia.

"No, no, not that! The other thing!" she yelped.

"Oh yeah, I asked you what you liked to do," replied Mia.

"NO!" shouted Lilly.

"Oh, the sea animals?" smiled Mia.

"NO! NOT THAT! WHAT DID YOU SAY BEFORE WE SLEPT?" yelled Lilly at the top of her lungs, not caring about everyone now staring at her.

Mia did not look offended at all. She only chuckled at Lilly's face and said, "I said that the flight to Ocean Academy was at 7 o'clock."

"Umm..." went Chloe, "I hate to interrupt you two, but isn't it already 7'o clock?"

They stared at the clock in dismay. It was 7 o'clock, no doubt.

"Run!" Lilly shouted. "We have to save the mermaids!"

"Mermaids? I had a dream about mermaids. There was a clam and a golden pearl. There was also a war. I hated that part. It was scary," shivered Chloe. "Err, why are you both looking at me like that?"

Lilly and Mia quickly told Chloe about what they had to do. Chloe instantly understood and wanted to help. Chloe was also one of the chosen girls to find the Crystal Clam. The trio then ran and ran, jumping over suitcases, stumbling past trolleys and hurrying by some people. By the time they arrived at the plane, they were tired and sweaty.

(They could have been in a play and pretended that they'd just taken a shower. That was how sweaty they were.)

"That was tiring!" panted Mia.

"At least we're here," gasped Chloe.

"Come here, onto the plane," huffed Lilly.

But what a surprise! The plane flew off! It zoomed into the blue sky, without the girls! They stared in disbelief. But it had gone, and there was no turning back now.

"Argh!" complained Lilly. "We can't go! We're too late!"

"Oh, no!" yelled Mia.

"Hmm. We need a solution, we must help the mermaids," thought Chloe.

"And we need it quickly. We have to get on the plane, and we need to do it now!" shouted Lilly.

"Oooh, look!" said Mia, suddenly pointing to a bag.

The bag was bright red in colour and was glowing. Mia forced it open and there in the bag lay some things that were folded and dome shaped.

The other girls walked towards the 'dome shaped items'.

"What are they?" said Lilly curiously, tugging at the bag.

"I know!" said Chloe, gasping in joy. "They're parachutes! But why are the parachutes glowing?"

"I think I know why," said Lilly, and took the pearl out her pocket. "This is the pearl from the Crystal Clam. It's also glowing. It wants to show us the way."

"Wow! But I don't know how to activate a parachute. I've never used one," said Mia, scratching her head in confusion.

Lilly had never used a parachute either. However, Chloe had!

"I know how you use one! I've parachuted many times before," informed Chloe. "You put it on like this- no Mia! The other way around- yes! That's right. Then..."

Chloe had used parachutes a lot, and it was one of her favourite sports. She showed the girls how they worked and helped them put them on.

"You just pull this cord. It's called a drogue. This'll make the parachute open and then you steer by pulling these ropes," said Chloe. "Watch me first, then you go."

Chloe jumped and pulled her cord. Lilly heard a whoosh as Chloe's parachute flew up into the air. She watched in awe as she got higher and higher, whilst following the plane. She heard delighted cries and felt excitement tug at her toes.

Lilly felt that she wanted to jump too, but something made her feet stick to the ground.

She took deep breaths, but she heard whispers of fear.

"Umm, you can go first," said Lilly to Mia.

"OK, see you there!" said Mia.

Mia copied what Chloe did and was sensible for once. She followed the plane by pulling ropes in order to move and follow its direction.

She laughed with joy and didn't want to land. Lilly knew that she had to at least try. Ignoring her worries, she leapt high and pulled the cord. She felt a burst of wind in her face and swayed in the air.

Lilly glanced down and saw her feet dangling above the ground. She had done it!

The girls had now got the hang of parachuting and they could glide towards the plane. It was frightening, but also fun at the same time.

Ever got the feeling where you're on a rollercoaster? It's scary, but fun. That was exactly how they felt.

Since the girls had no way of getting into the plane, they had to parachute and follow it from behind.

"We can't parachute for this long!" wailed Lilly.

"Hmm. Let's go onto a wing of the plane," thought Mia.

"Yes, we can rest there," nodded Chloe.

The girls glided gracefully towards the plane, now equipped with newly learnt skills. Lilly landed firmly on the plane's left wing, and she sat down. Staring at the land below, she held on tightly and smiled.

She hung her parachute on the plane's wing, making sure it held still. With that done, she could lie back and watch the clouds drift in peace.

Now, if you actually go on a plane's wing, your head would most likely rip off because of the plane's speed. Either the girls were very strong, or I just had to make the girls able to sit on the plane so the storyline would continue nicely.

We shall have to skip an hour in the story, if you don't mind. Because that's when all the drama comes in …

Back to the story now!

One hour later…

WHOOSH!

"Erm, why is the plane being so loud?" asked Lilly.

"I'm not sure," replied Chloe.

"Either it's a fire-breathing dragon flying above us, a man-eating lion's inside the plane, or... WE'RE GOING TO LAND!" screamed Mia.

"AAAH!" they all shouted.

WHOOSH! WHOOSH! WHOOSH!

Lilly could feel the plane dipping down towards the ground.

She gasped worriedly and felt her long mop of hair being whipped from side to side. Mia was right!

They were going to land. Lilly instantly knew it would be dangerous, because they were literally sitting on the plane's wing.

They could get easily blown off. (She was so frightened that she would've preferred the lion or even the dragon.)

"HOLD ON!" screeched Lilly.

HELP!

The girls gripped onto the plane, clinging on like a troop of monkeys.

Swiftly, Lilly could feel herself slipping towards the edge of the plane's wing. She screamed and fought the urge to explode into pieces. (If she did explode, she would die. Also, Mia and Chloe would die too.)

Lilly slid further backwards. Her hands were starting to slip from the plane as she shut her eyes. She was falling and falling and falling...

"Phew!" said Mia and Chloe.

Lilly opened her eyes. She hadn't fallen off! Her hand had just been gotten caught on her parachute. She just had the sensation of falling.

If you didn't remember, Lilly had fastened her parachute on the side of the plane's wing! She pulled herself back up.

The plane suddenly got faster. Lilly ducked and held onto the wing as tightly as possible and once again closed her eyes. WHOOSH!

Lilly blinked. The plane had landed, and they were all safe! (Well, except that Lilly felt like she had broken her toe in the process.)

"Yay!" cheered the girls, feeling all happy and secure.

Lilly skidded off the plane and landed with a bump on the ground. She was safe, but only for now...

Chapter Four

A Letter

The girls walked inside the airport terminal after landing at the airport and noticed that their bags had arrived and were sitting on a luggage conveyor belt. Lilly wondered how the bags could get from one place to another.

"Now where do we go?" said Lilly.

"I'm not sure," said Chloe.

"I know!" said Mia.

"Where do we go then?" asked Lilly.

"Somewhere!" said Mia, bursting into peals of laughter.

Lilly and Chloe just sighed and rolled their eyes. Where did they need to go now?

"Maybe we need a bus?" thought Lilly.

"Hmm, lots of the children are over there at the bus stop. I think you're right Lilly," agreed Chloe.

Mia was already running towards the bus stop. A bus was already there waiting, and all of the children hopped onto it.

"Let's go, before we're late again!" called Mia. "I'm not going to parachute towards a bus!"

They got on the bus just in time, and the moment the girls were on and seated, that was the very moment the bus started to move!

Mia sat next to Chloe, but that meant Lilly had to sit somewhere else. She peered round the row of seats and sat beside another girl.

The girl had wavy brown hair, the colour of chestnuts. A sweatband firmly held her hair in place, though she didn't look sporty like Chloe.

Her skirt was short and green like a blade of grass in the early morning, and she had a smile upon her face. She clearly liked to cook, since there was a book on her lap called *Recipes to Share*.

"Hello! My name is Lucy," the girl introduced herself.

"Hi, I'm Lilly. They are my friends," said Lilly, and she pointed to Mia and Chloe.

"Nice. I'm excited to go to Ocean Academy!"

"Me too!"

"Though I had the weirdest dream, with mermaids and shadowy creatures!" Lucy confirmed, just like all the others had been experiencing.

"Woah! Hey, Mia, Chloe, come here," called Lilly.

They explained what they believed their mission was, and explained all about the Crystal Clam. All of a sudden, Lucy seemed serious and was willing to help as much as possible.

Now all four girls were sitting on the bus. Lilly and her friends were a proper team now, and they were determined to help the mermaids.

Lilly was still tired, seeing as she had almost died falling off a plane. She opened her suitcase to find her diary. It wasn't a huge one, she barely wrote anything in it really.

If you have a diary, and only write a little bit in it, have a look at Lilly's diary. You'll see how much you write compared to Lilly!

Lilly's (Tiny) Diary:

> I have met some friends. We parachuted to get to the plane. I almost fell off. Mia, stop looking over my shoulder as I am writing this. Bye.

See what I mean? So short! It also had few pages, and you obviously know why. But anyways, enough of diaries. We are not focusing on diaries in this story.

Besides, diaries are private. So I shouldn't be sharing this with you.

Soon, after a long and tiring trip on the bus, all of the children came to a sandy, golden beach. As Lilly stepped off the bus, the fresh, salty smell of the ocean came gushing in huge waves around herself. The sparkling sand made a crunching noise under her feet as she took each step. There was a woman sitting in a rowing boat, and she looked like she was waiting for them all to arrive.

The woman was wearing a long-sleeved, silky top, and deep purple trousers. She also had round glasses with thick rims. Though she wore something on her head that looked like a piece of cloth. *It's hot at the moment, she should take that off. I'll ask her later,* thought Lilly.

"Hello dear children, and welcome to Ocean Academy. My name is Miss Jannah, and I am your headteacher," she explained cheerfully, smiling at everyone.

Lilly felt her eyes widen as big as saucepans and she fought the resisting urge to run around shouting, "YAY!"

"This beach is certainly not the school, if you were thinking that! Do you see those dots in the distance?" Miss Jannah continued, pointing to the sea. "Those are the other boats, and the other teachers are on them. We will row to Ocean Academy. Only three on a boat, including teachers!"

A few minutes later, the boats came to shore. They were all identical; wooden and strong.

The children stepped onto them, and Lilly sat with Lucy. Lilly sighed, feeling relieved. The sea was vast and beautiful!

She loved staring at the depths of the crystal clear, blue waters, so clear that she could see some fish swimming beneath the ocean waves. The girl put her hand in the water; it felt refreshing and cool. Seagulls squawked up high, perhaps seeking out lunch.

"It seems that you like the sea!" said Miss Jannah, who was on the boat with them.

"Yes, very much," said Lilly, nodding her head.

"That's good, because we're going to have lots of sea activities, like surfing and swimming. We will also be enjoying some seafood," said Miss Jannah.

"I also have a question," said Lilly.

"Yes?" said Miss Jannah.

"What is that thing on your head? The weather's so hot! You must be even hotter! Maybe you should take it off," said Lilly, and pointed to the cloth on Miss Jannah's head.

"This is called a headscarf. I am a Muslim, and I must wear it," said Miss Jannah.

"Is that a different religion?" asked Lilly.

"Well, it's called Islam," replied Miss Jannah.

"Isn't it hot?" queried Lilly.

"At first, of course it's hot. But then you get used to it," said the headteacher.

Lilly studied Miss Jannah's headscarf, which was light purple, so it matched her trousers. It also had a pretty, pink flower. Lilly liked her caring personality.

Lilly nodded and went back to rowing. Rowing was hard and heavy work. You had to push and pull these things called oars back and forth, which made the boat move forward.

Not long after about an hour, when they were at the school, *oh goodness me,* how surprised the children were! The school was built on wooden platforms, like the leaflet had said. There was a huge building in the middle, and coming out from the building, were bridges. These bridges led to what looked like other platforms with houses!

Other bridges led to other buildings, which were most likely places by where the students could eat or play.

All of the children came to one of the platforms to tie the boats to the pier. There were wooden posts and strings on the platforms. All you had to do was simply tie a string to your boat!

"We will need to arrange you into your dorms. The four dorms are, Sapphire, Ruby, Emerald and Diamond. As you can see," Miss Jannah said, pointing in the distance. "Those houses are all grouped into whatever colour their gem is, like where Ruby dorm houses are red. Reach into the bag that I am holding, and your dorm shall be revealed. In your dorm groups, you will all try to earn points. The dorm with the most points at the end of the term will receive their next term for free!"

Lilly then stepped forwards, far too excited to let others pick from the bag first. She pulled something out of the silk bag. Surprisingly, it was a sweet. Mmm. She opened up it's wrapper and saw a green gleam. That probably meant she was in Emerald dorm.

Popping the sweet into her mouth, Miss Jannah ushered her towards the green row of houses.

A thought suddenly nagged at her. What if her friends weren't in the same dorm as her? But then she felt a warm glow. She suddenly felt inside her pocket, and saw the pearl. The pearl was glowing and she saw that the bag of sweets glowed golden whenever her friends had to choose a sweet. *I mustn't worry*, said Lilly to herself. *The pearl will help me.* Even so, Lilly could not help feeling herself fidget slightly.

Luckily, she spotted her friends sauntering towards her.

"Hooray!" cheered Lilly. A speaker attached to one of the houses let out a loud noise. "This is Miss Jannah speaking here! The houses that are the colour of the dorm you are in, are for you! You will be staying in the houses and you shall choose three other children to stay in a house with you!"

Lilly and her friends walked towards a house with the best view of the sea, but another girl pushed them out of their way.

The girl had pitch-black hair and a yellow dress. She seemed extremely posh and arrogant, due to the smug expression on her face. Also, she stood with a gang of snooty-looking friends.

"Excuse me, out the way," she said.

"Yeah, out the way," echoed her friends.

"No, *you* go out the way. We were here first, and don't even try to push us," said Mia.

"No! I was here first!" grumbled the girl.

"Yeah! She was here first!" repeated the gang.

"Liar! We're staying here," huffed Mia.

"By the way, I'm Megan," she spat.

"Yeah! She's Megan," added Megan's friends.

"Zip it, you sillies!" screamed Megan, glaring at her gang.

"Zip it you sill- oh wait, we're the sillies," mumbled Megan's gang, stepping backwards.

"Don't try to change the subject! Clear off!" shouted Mia.

Megan sashayed grumpily to another house, whilst Mia rudely stuck out her tongue.

"That'll teach her," said Mia in triumph.

Lilly instantly knew that Megan was someone to watch out for. Megan probably never spoke nicely, something that Lilly hated.

The girls strolled into the wooden, firm house. There were no stairs, so the house was cosy like a burrow.

There were beds with plump cushions and one wardrobe for each of them to use. A pale green rug sat on the floor, and another door led to a bathroom. A clock hung on the wall and a speaker (probably for Miss Jannah to easily contact them) was next to it.

Almost all at once, they began unpacking and settling in. Lilly piled her clothes neatly in the wardrobe, placed her toothbrush in the bathroom and finally lay down on her bed. She then decided to go for a short walk.

She skipped happily along the pier, and saw Megan with another girl. This other girl had brown skin, dark hair and a nice smile.

"Hi!" said the girl. "My name is Fatima. That's Megan."

"She knows that I'm Megan," huffed Megan grumpily.

"Anyways, we're collecting rubbish in the sea," explained Fatima. "It's so important to keep our oceans safe. Otherwise creatures like this turtle can get stuck

in the rubbish. Poor thing."
Lilly felt sorry for the sea
turtle. The girls soon
decided to take it to a
teacher.

"Right, I'll take it to the
teachers," declared Megan. "And
Fatima is correct. We must save the seas. There's
also lots of global warming nowadays, meaning
that the world is getting hotter! This means that
icebergs up North are cracking, and polar bears
don't have anywhere to live. Then when all the
icebergs melt, the sea level rises. Imagine Ocean
Academy sinking!"

Lilly nodded, realizing that keeping the oceans
safe was very important! She went back to the
dormitory, and also thought that Megan and
Fatima were kind people; they wanted to help the
sea!

Lilly opened the door- and something smacked
right into her face!

"Ow!" yelped Lilly.

She spotted an envelope on her lap. Like the pearl, the envelope was wrapped in seaweed! An envelope had hit her, but why? Envelopes don't appear out of nowhere, as you all know. The other girls shuffled over to have a look at the green envelope. Lilly held her breath and teared it open, chucking the seaweed in the bin on the other side of the room. Inside was... nothing!

"Is this a joke?" said Lilly, feeling annoyed.

"What do you mean? There's a letter in your hand," said Chloe, pointing at Lilly.

"Huh?" said Lilly, staring at her hand.

Hmm, there *was* a letter in her hand. How strange! It had swirly, posh handwriting, which was a complete puzzle to read.

She read it out loud...

Dear Lilly, Mia, Chloe and Lucy,

You have arrived at Ocean Academy at last. I am Queen Maia, the ruler of Mermaid Lagoon.

Mermaid Lagoon lived in peace, in happiness, in harmony. At least until the Shadow Realm came along. They would steal mermaids to take as slaves.

One day they did manage to get full control of the Lagoon. They did this by throwing the Crystal Clam into your land, which mermaids call: The Terrifying Land Of Humans. (What? It is rather terrifying.) The clam is a legendary object we have. This clam keeps the Lagoon from turning evil, no matter what others do. But then, once it was gone, all hope was lost. Then I chanted that spell, to make sure the clam was delivered to a safe location. You all know this story from the dreams I sent you, remember?

The Shadow Realm have sent one of their most cunning spies to go to Ocean Academy and find the Crystal Clam.

These are the only things I know about the spy:

- The spy is a female child

- She is in your dorm

- She is clever and strong

- She has a power but I don't know what her power is

Speaking of powers, all of you have powers too. Your powers will be based on water, like making it rain or controlling currents. I have given you a book about powers so you can find out yours.

You must find clues to find the Crystal Clam. I have provided you with the first clue, which is:

Cooking is a talent for all, whether you be big or you be small. Volunteer at this challenge, choose a cake, you'll find the next clue in this thing to bake. When the cake is ready, take the first bite, you'll know what to do when the moon shines bright.

It may not make any sense now, but trust me, you will figure it out. Once you have the clam, hop in the water and shout, "I AM A MERMAID!". This will send you to Mermaid Lagoon.
Be careful! Watch out for the spy!
Best of luck, Queen Maia.

"Wow," said Lilly.

They read the letter over and over again, just to make sure that they understood every single word (and also because Queen Maia's handwriting was quite tricky to read). But then, Lilly noticed a face peeking through the window! She tried to identify who it was, but it was covered with a dark hood. Then just as quick as it arrived, it disappeared. The figure dashed away, so they couldn't see her.

"That must have been the spy," shivered Lilly.

All of a sudden, the speaker shook violently and yelled, "Miss Jannah here! It is lunch soon! Who would like to volunteer to help the cooks make lunch? Two children from each dorm please!"

"Hey," said Lilly. "One of us should go and help!"

"Why?" asked Lucy.

"Because it's *cooking!* The Queen said the first challenge was to do with cooking! And a cake! So one of us should go, and volunteer to cook a cake for dessert!" shouted Lilly.

"Yes, but if the spy is smart, won't she be there too?" said Chloe.

"Then we just need to keep a low profile. I should go!" said Mia. "Because I know how to spy. I spy all the time. I ate all the hidden chocolates by sneaking in the storage room. I spoilt my sis's cooking by swapping sugar with salt. I even found out my birthday present months ago by-"

"Actually, I think I should go," said Lucy. "I'm good at cooking. Then I can volunteer to make dessert."

"So it's settled then," said Lilly. "Let's go, and we'll find that spy!"

72

Chapter Five

Wet Cake

"OK! We will make a simple dish, a mix of seafood!" shouted the chef.

"Yes, Chef!" the children shouted back.

Lilly shivered. How was a mix of seafood simple? She herself, was not that good at cooking, and she usually burnt a part of whatever she was cooking.

Well, really, I mean burnt the whole thing.

Lilly, Mia and Chloe were watching the hardworking children cook. If Lucy was able to cook something nice, maybe the chef would allow her to bake a cake for dessert. Then they would be able to find the next clue!

They peered at Lucy as she cooked. All that could be heard was sizzling and shouting! *Just CHAOS!*

Lilly saw that Lucy was trying her hardest. She was so careful and precise! So precise, that Lilly thought she could cook for ten Gordon Ramseys. (The best chef in the world!)

Until... Megan pushed her.

Megan roughly shoved Lucy. Lucy managed to stand up but she dropped a bottle of oil. The oil went tumbling to the ground, and Lucy just stared at it. All of the oil had seeped onto her shoes.

"Hey!" yelped Lucy. "You spilt the oil on my shoes!"

Her shoes were now not their usual pretty black. Instead, they were black and smelly. There was now utter chaos in the kitchen, smelly black shoes, a puddle of oil, and a smirking Megan.

"Not my fault," sneered Megan, sticking her tongue out.

"Lucy! Why did you spill the oil?

Minus ten points to Emerald dorm!" boomed the chef, hands on her hips.

"Sorry, Chef," mumbled Lucy, even though it wasn't her fault.

"Baa baa black shoes, why are you smelly?" teased Megan, laughing and pointing.

Baa baa black shoes, why are you smelly?

Lilly felt sorry for her friend. It wasn't her fault! Lucy then sidled over to them. "Sorry," she said. "Megan pushed me."

"It's not your fault," said Lilly.

"Yeah, so get Megan back," said Mia.

"Or tell the cook that it was Megan," said Chloe.

"Thanks girls, but I don't know how to turn back time. Besides, I hate snitching. What can I do? No-one else spilt anything," she sighed, going back to the pot of squid.

Lilly had to do something. But she didn't want oil spilt on her shoes. She groaned and decided to read the book from Queen Maia.

She decided to read a section that told you about which power you'd most likely get.

Powers are something to be taken care of. They depend on your personality.

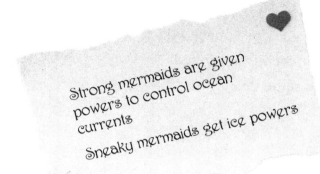

Strong mermaids are given powers to control ocean currents

Sneaky mermaids get ice powers

Lilly kept reading. Nothing for Lucy yet. Until her eyes rested on the last sentence...

Mermaids who love to cook are given the ability to heat water

She went to a page which gave information all about heating water. It was very helpful, and it gave some useful tips.

1. Find some water (or there is nothing to heat up).

2. Stare at the water. Don't blink.

3. The water will heat up.

4. Blink once you are done.

Note: This power can be used to heat water until the water disappears. You also cannot undo the actions of this power. Once you have heated the water, there is no undoing it. Unless you use new water, of course.

Lilly jabbed her finger on the book and let Lucy read it.

"Wow!" gasped Lucy. "But how will I use this power to help me?"

"When you need to heat some water, use your magic. The others will be taking longer to heat their water, while you've already done yours.

The chef is bound to notice that you are doing your work quickly, while you are actually using magic! Then ask if you can make a cake, and maybe the chef will say yes," explained Lilly.

Lucy agreed to her plan. So when they were required to heat some water, Lucy took a deep breath. She stared hard. A mist formed in her eyes, and the pot started to shake. It was heating up! Once it had finished, Lucy blinked and got back to cooking.

"Good job, Lucy. You're working very fast today. Ten points to Emerald dorm," commented the chef.

"Thank you, Chef," smiled Lucy.

"Would you like to bake dessert?"

"OK, Chef."

"Can I bake a cake, Chef?" asked Megan quickly. "I can help Lucy."

"OK," responded the chef.

The four friends were all frozen to the spot.

How could Megan know about the cake? Or was it just a coincidence?

Lilly was just about to go and shout right in Megan's face, but she fought the resisting urge to do so. What if she wasn't the spy? Then it would be hard to explain.

"Hello?" said Megan impatiently. "Are we going to start?"

"OK, let's bake a cake," said Lucy.

"Do you know any good recipes for a cake then?" said Megan.

"Hmm, I'm not quite sure. I don't usually bake cakes. Let's Google a recipe then," said Lucy.

So Lucy and Megan tried to
search up a good recipe.
They found a Moist Vanilla
Cupcake recipe by
Apron4Two on Instagram.

Hello there. Apron4Two isn't made up in this
story! It's real! I have included the recipe at the
end of this book.

Don't forget to check it out!

Right, back to the story...

"Oooh, let's do this one, it looks good," said
Lucy.

"OK," said Megan.

The pair baked the cakes
with great accuracy. Lucy
also kept an eye out for any
clues, but there wasn't anything to consider.
Lilly couldn't detect anything either.

81

Once the cakes were ready, Lucy darted forwards to grab it. She had to get the first bite! Megan was trying to get it too.

Did that mean that she was the spy? Or did she just *want* some cake? Everybody likes cake. Megan's hand reached forwards, but Lucy managed to clasp her fingers first around a crumb and popped it in her mouth.

Megan's mouth looked as if she had eaten a sour lemon, frowning as though with wrinkles that resembled an elephant's head. But when she saw Lucy looking, she forced a smile.

After cooking, all of the children sat down to eat. Lilly had never tried seafood before (except fish), and she found out that it was rather delicious. She gobbled it up happily, licking the sauce off her fingers.

"OK, the cake is done, and Lucy had the first bite. But then how do we find out the clue?" said Lilly.

"I guess we'll find out at night if the moon comes out," said Chloe.

"The moon *will* come out. I know it," said Mia.

"But Megan was acting strangely. I mean, she wanted to help but she doesn't like us," said Lucy.

"Do you think she's the spy?" asked Lilly.

"She must be! What other reason could there be for trying to get the cake?" said Mia.

"No, she can't be! She really wants to keep the seas safe!" said Lilly.

"Well, we're ahead. Whoever this spy is, she won't find out the clue," said Lucy.

"Let's wait and see," said Chloe. "If we don't do anything suspicious, maybe we can trick the spy."

And with that being said, they finished their lunch and went off to lessons. Lessons were actually not that boring. There were a few fun lessons, like fishing.

Lilly found that she liked to fish, because you could just sit and chat to your friends whilst waiting for some fish to swim along.

At the end of the day, they were waiting outside for the moon to come out. Lilly stared at the sky in hope, twiddling her thumbs.

"Look!" said Lilly. "The moon!"

Right there was the moon, big and bright! But a curious thing happened. The moon was slowly turning into a light brown-ish colour, and then it shrank!

"It looks just like the cake that I baked with Megan!" said Lucy.

The moon fell into the water, looking exactly like a cake! A cloaked figure, not much larger than themselves, ran up to the moon/cake.

(Let's call it a moon cake.)

The figure could not get into the water, and neither could they.

"What will we do? That figure, who is obviously the spy, will just be after us!" said Mia.

The mysterious figure glared at them. Lilly caught a tiny glimpse of the spy's face, but she couldn't see who it was. She was sure the figure was a girl though.

The only thing Lilly was able to identify was that the spy had black hair.

"Look! Let's row!" screeched Lilly, pointing to the boats they used to reach Ocean Academy.

The girls went into pairs of two, and began to row. The figure saw what they were doing and tried to copy them. But it was hard for the spy to row on her own. Lilly was with Chloe, who was quite skilled at rowing, so they managed to get to the moon cake first. She pulled it out of the water and cheered happily.

But the figure's eyes glowed red. Suddenly, a ferocious, pitch-black gorilla appeared and swam menacingly towards them, nostrils flared! Lilly had heard that gorillas were very strong, and she didn't want to get hurt.

"Change of plans!" said Lilly, trembling. "What if we give you half of the cake?"

"Good," said the unidentified figure, but then took most of the cake!

"Not fair!" yelped Lilly.

They returned to Emerald dorm. There was no point in trying to retrieve the cake, otherwise the gorilla could hurt them.

Lilly looked at the soggy, sickening cake. The girls suddenly heard a voice.

"Every bite of the cake you must take, you won't find the clue until you finish your plate," whispered the voice.

"Hold on, we have to eat *this?*" spluttered Mia.

"Yuck! It smells," choked Lucy.

"But what about the spy's piece of cake?" thought Chloe.

"I don't know, but we need to try. It might work," shivered Lilly.

How unlucky for the girls! The cake did not taste nice at all. It was as if you were putting raw fish and mud from a swamp into your mouth.

The texture of the cake was slimy, so slimy that Lilly had a sudden thought about the cake actually being a frog. At least the spy had taken more of the cake, so they did not need to eat as much.

Lilly hated the cake. It was perfect, but with one imperfection; it was like it was dipped in saltwater. Shovelling the cake in her mouth, Lilly hoped that she wouldn't be physically sick afterwards.

"Right, we've finished! Phew!" gasped Lilly, sighing in relief.

"Right, I've got some milk," smiled Lucy, giving everyone a glass.

"Now we have to wait for the clue," grinned Chloe, gulping down the milk with great pleasure.

"Yes. But I can still taste the cake in my mouth. Now I'll never eat cake again," joked Mia, laughing heartily.

In the blink of an eye, the crumbs of the cake all paranormally joined together like a puzzle! They glowed brightly and shone like stars. The crumbs then fell to the ground, but now combined, they formed the shape of a letter.

It looked like a letter from Queen Maia, due to the fancy handwriting on it.

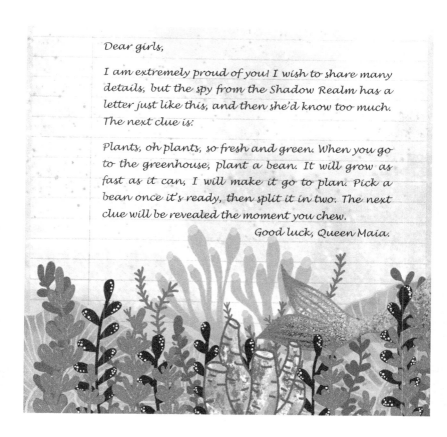

Dear girls,

I am extremely proud of you! I wish to share many details, but the spy from the Shadow Realm has a letter just like this, and then she'd know too much. The next clue is:

Plants, oh plants, so fresh and green. When you go to the greenhouse, plant a bean. It will grow as fast as it can, I will make it go to plan. Pick a bean once it's ready, then split it in two. The next clue will be revealed the moment you chew.

Good luck, Queen Maia.

"Right," said Lilly, "we need to plant a bean!"

Chapter Six

Jack and the Beanstalk

"Good morning!" said Lilly, skipping around. "I can't wait to find the next clue!"

"Ha! Someone's excited!" said Mia, laughing.

A loud voice came booming out from the speaker, "Good morning children! Come and eat breakfast! We will also have gardening today! After will be maths!"

"Gardening?" said Chloe. "We could plant a bean!"

"Yes!" said Lucy. "But make sure the spy doesn't get it. What are our clues about the spy again?"

Lilly had written some notes about what they knew about the spy:

1. She is female.

2. She is in our dorm.

3. Her powers include making a gorilla appear.

4. She is clever and strong.

5. She has black hair.

So after breakfast, all of the students went to the greenhouse to plant some flowers and vegetables. Lilly clutched a sachet of seeds and raced over to the soil.

"We can catch the spy in the act! I do this all the time at home. Like when my sweets are gone, and then I find out who it is!" said Mia.

"How can we figure out who the spy is?" said Lucy.

"Yes, how? It's not like we can ask anyone," said Chloe.

"The spy will also be planting a bean," said Mia, "so if anyone plants a bean, they could be the spy!"

"Oh, good idea!" said Lilly.

Unfortunately, many people were in the same location planting beans. It seemed as though beans were quite popular. (This was surprising to Lilly, because she hated beans.)

Slightly worried, she then decided to make a suspects list, to at least try to identify who the spy could be.

1. Sita
2. Tom
3. Olivia
4. Fatima
5. Joe
6. Megan
7. Grace

"That's a lot of suspects!" said Lilly.

"Let's cross off the boys, because the suspect is a girl," said Mia.

"That means we now have Sita, Olivia, Megan and Grace," said Lucy.

"Now we need to cross off the ones with hair that isn't black, because the suspect has black hair," said Chloe.

"That leaves Fatima, Megan and Grace," said Lilly.

"Now, which ones aren't in our dorm?" said Mia.

"Hmm, Fatima and Megan are in Emerald dorm, Grace isn't," said Lucy.

"Good. Next, which one can make a gorilla appear?" said Chloe.

"Err, how are we meant to know that?" said Mia.

"OK, which one is clever and strong then?" said Chloe.

"They're both strong. Look, they're both pushing wheelbarrows full of fruit," said Lilly.

"Which of them is clever?" asked Lucy.

"We don't know," said Mia.

Hmm. Not good. This was a hard question. Which was more clever?

"Eureka!" yelled Mia.

"Eureka? What does that even mean?" asked Chloe.

"It means she has an idea. What's your idea, Mia?" questioned Lucy.

"My idea is that... you can think of an idea, while I go to the next lesson, which is maths. Even though I hate maths," replied Mia.

"Not helping!" sighed Chloe.

"Wait, good idea!" gasped Lilly.

"Huh? My idea is good? Oh wait, yes, of course it's good," muttered Mia.

"Maths is the next lesson, like you said, Mia. So we could change some questions in their maths books!" said Lilly. "Make them hard questions.

Whoever gets the most questions correct will be the spy!"

So fifteen minutes before the maths lesson was to begin, the girls crept quietly to the classroom. Lilly quietly opened the door and peered around. There was no-one! She then spotted Fatima and Megan's maths books in a neat pile. She grabbed the books and furiously started writing.

"Let's change the questions!" hissed Lilly.

(Easy) Original Questions:

$$5 \times 4 =$$

$$8 \times 3 =$$

$$3 \times 5 =$$

(Very Hard) Changed Questions:

    564x4=

    832x3=

    374x5=

This took ages to do, because Lilly had to try and copy the original handwriting instead of her usual style.

"Good, this should work," declared Lilly. "The questions are much harder than the previous ones. I'm not even sure how to solve them myself."

During maths, Lilly sat between Fatima and Megan. She gazed at their work and tried to see what they were doing. Fatima wasn't having much luck.

"564 x 4? How can I do that?" she thought, peering at the questions.

On the other hand, Megan wasn't having any trouble at all.

Maths

564 × 4 = 2256

832 × 3 = 2496

347 × 5 = 1735

Megan

"Finished!" she shouted, waving her book in the air.

"Wait. So the suspect is... Megan!" the girls all said.

Lilly saw it all. Of course it was Megan! She had tried to get that cake, she wasn't nice to them, *she* was the one who was trying to stop them!

"What are you girls talking about?" said Megan suspiciously, walking up to them.

"Nothing, err, nothing," said Lilly. But Megan wasn't fooled easily.

"Who cares if you know I'm the spy? The first time I saw you, I already knew you were helping Mermaid Lagoon. You'll never find the Crystal Clam! It's mine, and you call yourselves spies? Ha! If only you knew the true story," she scoffed, walking away, albeit with a sad face.

"True story? She just wants to trick us," said Mia.

This made Lilly think.

Was Megan really trying to trick us? She looked a bit sad when she said those last words. And she cares about the sea! Should I tell the others? What if I'm wrong? Then I'll just look silly, she thought.

So she decided to keep it to herself.

Megan obviously cared about the sea. Could that mean she was trying to trick them? Or was it only because she had lived underwater, in the Shadow Realm?

There were many possible answers.

Was Megan good?

Was Megan someone nice?

Or... was it all a lie?

The next day, the girls went to check on the beans. As Queen Maia had told them, the beans would grow quickly, so everyone's beans were tall like skyscrapers. Lilly stared up at the beanstalks.

They looked as if they would go on forever. They even went into the misty, white clouds.

It was all quite peculiar. Queen Maia had said the beanstalks would grow high, but Lilly wasn't expecting to see plants *this high!* From the bottom, it was an amazing sight!

Though from the top, I don't think I could say the same...

"Woah! It's like Jack and the Beanstalk!" said Lilly, touching the beanstalk's leaves.

"More like Four Girls and the Beanstalk!" laughed Mia, pointing at all her friends.

"I don't get it," mumbled Chloe, not understanding.

"Hey, we can climb the beanstalk!" gasped Lucy, hopping onto the plant.

Strange, they *could* climb it. It was like a massive tower, but green. She almost expected to find a giant at the top.

"Hey, Megan's climbing *her* beanstalk!" said Chloe.

Chloe was right. Megan was climbing up her own beanstalk, trying to reach one of her beans.

"Come on, we need to get a bean too!" said Lucy.

It was a right struggle to get up the beanstalk! The stalk itself was slippery, which made the girls fall straight to the ground. The only safe place on the slippery structure were the leaves, because they were soft like pillows. To add to that, the beanstalks were so high that they reached up into the clouds! It was very windy at the top, so Lilly was in danger of falling.

Uh oh... Lilly thought. *It's sort of high... Don't look*

down! Don't look down! Don't look- Help! I shouldn't have looked!

Mia then began to sing. It really wasn't helping. "Beans, beans, good for the heart! The more you eat, the more you-"

Beans, beans, good for the heart!

"Stop singing! Besides, that song's rude," remarked the girls.

Once they reached one of the beans (and once Mia had stopped singing), they were panting with effort. Lilly desperately tried to pull the bean. It was stuck like glue, and wouldn't budge.

It seemed as if it had been stuck for absolutely ages, since it wouldn't move one bit.

"It won't come off!" screeched Lilly, sighing in frustration.

"OK, on three, we pull," declared Mia, taking charge.

"One, two, three… PULL!" the girls shouted.

They pulled the bean with all their might. It started to slightly come off the beanstalk and leaned towards the girls. But then, Lilly felt a sharp push. It was the bean. Well, not the bean, a *falling bean!*

"AAAH!" screamed Lilly.

She slid down the beanstalk, the bean rolling behind her.

She remembered the story Alice In Wonderland and pictured herself with a blue dress, sliding past a huge-sized bean. It was bumpy and uncomfortable, but Lilly thought a rough ride was better than being squashed by a massive bean.

Lilly suddenly remembered something else. *What did she read in that book from the Queen?*

"MIA!" yelled Lilly. "I READ THAT SNEAKY MERMAIDS HAVE ICE POWERS! POINT AT THE BEAN TO FREEZE IT!"

Lilly had to shout as loud as she could, because she was a long way from her friends. Also, Mia wasn't the best at following orders.

Luckily, Mia was sensible and assertive in this moment. She narrowed her eyes and pointed directly at the humongous bean.

An icy mist spurted out and flew onto the bean. Lilly froze. Well, *she* didn't freeze, the *bean* did!

"Yay!" cheered Mia.

Lilly slid further down, her friends following her. She greeted them all with a hug and a smile. She also couldn't help laughing a little at Megan, who was sliding on her bean in a lopsided and somewhat farcical way.

"We're not done yet. We still have to cut the bean in two," said Lilly. "How are we supposed to cut it? It's frozen."

Lucy used her magic to heat the ice. The bean came rolling down. It tumbled faster and faster, gaining speed at each second.

BANG!

The bean hit the ground and instantly split into two. Small fragments of it flew into the air and landed near Lilly's feet.

Then they each hesitantly took a small bite. Surprisingly, it tasted like a vanilla cake.

Lilly only took the tiniest bit that she could. Not because she didn't like beans, but because the cake flavour reminded her of the soggy cake from yesterday.

Suddenly, the rest of the bean shrank into the size of a letter. Lilly recognized that handwriting. It was from Queen Maia.

Dear girls,

Good job! Unfortunately, the spy has got the same letter too. But well done for finding out who she is!

The next clue is:

Surfing, what fun! A thing to do for everyone. Courage is needed, high places to go. Once you're there, surf with the flow! After that, ride the waves. Inside it is where the next clue stays.

Hope you can do it (which you will!)

Queen Maia.

"Oooh, surfing!" gasped Chloe.

"How do you even surf?" asked Mia.

"No idea," sighed Lucy.

"Well, we'll find out!" grinned Lilly.

Chapter Seven

Surfing

"Hello children! Our special lesson for today is surfing!" blared the speaker.

Lilly opened her eyes. A beam of sunlight was blinding her eyes. It was the next day, and this time they were going to surf! Clever Queen Maia, always knowing what would happen next!

So after breakfast (which was some toast), the girls headed out. Mrs Smith, who was going to help them surf, was waiting for them. They were each given a surfboard and were going to learn to surf.

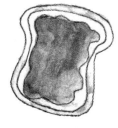

(Terribly Long) Surfing Method:

1. First, attach a leash to your surfboard. A leash is to keep you and your surfboard together.

2. Next, practice paddling on the ground. (By paddling on the ground, I mean *pretending* to paddle.)

3. Then, rub some wax onto the surfboards for better grip. Then paddle out properly onto the sea.

4. Once you have mastered that, you have to catch a wave. (No, that doesn't mean chasing a wave.) This means paddling towards a wave and then standing up.

5. After, surf! Keep your feet planted on the board, knees bent and arms loose.

6. Then, (oh gosh, it's complicated, isn't it!) try turning.

7. Finally, jump off the board when the waves die down, then paddle back to shore.

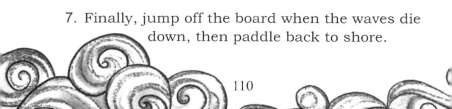

Oh dear, that was a long method of surfing! Surfing isn't easy. Lilly wasn't having a lot of luck either. But she got better and stopped falling into the water.

Chloe, on the other hand, was dashing her way through to the higher and higher waves. A huge wave then unexpectedly rose out of the sea. It roared violently and reached up to the sky.

"Chloe, ride that wave! *You know what* could be there!" shouted Lilly, trying not to reveal the idea of the Crystal Clam.

"OK," said Chloe, and she went to Mrs Smith. "Can I ride that wave?"

"OK, but be careful," said Mrs Smith.

Chloe paddled towards the humongous wave. It sounded like a motorbike's engine, and was the darkest blue. Still, she hopped onto her surfboard and stood up bravely.

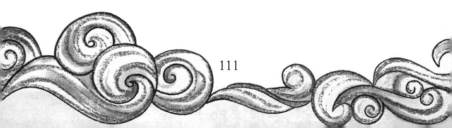

In no more than a minute, Chloe was surfing the biggest wave she had ever seen.

"Get to the top, Chloe!" yelled her friends, jumping up and down like hysterical monkeys.

So Chloe got higher and higher, and was soon practically on the side of the wave.

She balanced precariously, and it looked as if she was climbing a blue wall.

Chloe looked around and spotted a box right in front of her! It was studded with pearls and it glowed in the sunlight.

But a dreadful sight met her eyes. Megan was surfing right behind her! Megan was a surprisingly good surfer, almost as good as Chloe herself!

"Ha!" cackled Megan, and she clicked her fingers.

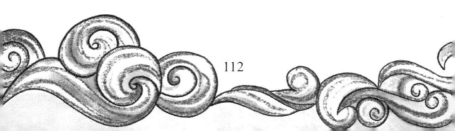

This made a grumpy, monstrous ogre float in front of Chloe. It had an axe, and seemed ready for battle.

"AAH!" yelped Chloe, and she lost her balance. She almost fell into the sea, but she was able to stand up. She took a deep breath and tried to replace her footing.

"Grr!" growled Megan.

Lilly saw that Chloe was done for. She would be crushed by the wave if she fell off. And Megan was certainly not making it any better.

Lilly reached out for the book about powers. Chloe was good at sports, so what powers did a sporty mermaid (or human, in this case) have?

- Friendly mermaids possess rain powers
- Confident mermaids carry ocean current powers
- Sporty mermaids have bubble powers

Lilly looked at that sentence that you just saw. Chloe had bubble powers! She decided to read about that power.

Flipping the pages of the book, she quickly scanned her eyes down the page in no more than a few seconds.

1. Clasp your hands together.
2. Open your hands up slowly.
3. A bubble will appear.
4. Push the bubble to where you want it to go.

Note: You can make bigger bubbles by clasping your hands together for a longer period of time. Bubbles can also be used to build things, like bridges. You can also use them to grab objects.

Lilly grabbed the book and stuck a piece of driftwood into the page about bubble magic, so it was like a bookmark. She then used all her strength to hurl the book towards Chloe. It zoomed through the air like a bird, and landed in Chloe's hands. Chloe's eyes scanned down the page and grinned.

She put her hands together and then took them apart. A bubble the size of her surfboard floated in its place. Chloe then gently pushed it towards the fancy box. It trapped the box inside itself, and went back to her.

"Yay!" cried Chloe.

"Yay!" cried the others.

"No!" cried Megan.

Afterwards, Chloe swam back to shore, the box in one hand.

"Well done!" smiled Lilly. "We can investigate this further at the end of the day in our dorm. Then we won't be disturbed."

But Megan was smiling. She was rubbing her hands together in greed, chuckling to herself. She was writing something in a book, but when the girls looked at her, she instantly stopped. Megan speedily ran away, but as she ran, she accidentally dropped her book.

"Eh? Why in the world is she doing that? I mean, she just lost!" yelled Mia.

"Be quiet! Megan might notice that she dropped her book!" shushed Chloe.

"Let's look inside it!" whispered Lucy.

The girls headed over to where Megan previously stood. Lilly read out loud the part that their enemy had just written.

Dear Diary,

The girls got the box from the clue! Chloe discovered her powers and now they are winning! I must do something. But I have an idea!

I will chase them once they go back to their dorm at sunset. I shall then find a way to get that box!

Wish me luck, Megan.

The girls gasped. Megan was going to try and ambush them!

"Well, we shall ambush *her!*" shouted Mia.

"How do we even do that?" queried Lucy.

"Erm, I don't know," admitted Mia.

"Telling us to ambush Megan and you don't know how," sighed Chloe.

Lucy then pulled a small book out of her pocket. (Yes, out of her pocket! That was how small it was. But it was very fat.)

"This is my diary," said Lucy.

> Dear Diary,
> I saw a pin on a piece of string.
> Hmm. Then I tried to grab it but I accidentally pushed it.
> The pin slid along the string and poked open a bag of
> marshmallows! There was also a note saying:
> HAPPY BIRTHDAY!
> I had forgotten it was my birthday all along!
> See ya later, Lucy.

"How will that even help?" asked Mia.

"Mia's right, how is your diary meant to help?" added Chloe.

"I'm right? Cool, I thought you'd never say that-oh wait, of course I'm right, I'm always right," bragged Mia.

"The marshmallow part! It was a trap," said Lucy.

"Make a trap and then use marshmallows? That's silly," said Mia.

Mmm!

"So what you're saying is, that we set a trap?" questioned Lilly.

"Yep," declared Lucy.

PING! An idea suddenly made its way into Lilly's head. She had the perfect idea for a trap. It was so simple, but it would work!

The girls got to work.

You will see what will happen. Be patient.

They connected some rope between Megan's dorm, over the sea, then to their own dorm. Lilly held a pair of scissors, whilst everyone else held some towels. She stood back and admired their handy-work. It was ready. So, at sunset, they pretended to stroll casually, as if they didn't know Megan's plot.

Megan suddenly jumped out of the shadows and clenched her fists.

"Give me the box!" roared Megan.

"Run!" Lilly called out.

They darted into Megan's dorm and clutched the towels. Lilly rushed desperately to the window, where the start of the rope was. She flung her towel over the rope and grabbed both ends as tightly as she could.

"GO!" yelled her friends.

It was now or never!

Lilly pushed off the window, using the towel to secure herself onto the rope, just like a zipline!

"Woo hoo!" cheered Lilly.

Her friends followed her and zoomed like eagles. On the other hand, Megan just looked more angry than ever. She growled like a lion and folded her arms.

What did you say, reader? Oh, you want to know how this is a trap? You shall see!

"Having trouble?" teased Mia, clearly enjoying the moment.

Lilly climbed off the rope and leapt into her dorm's window, where she was finally safe. She saw her friends climbing in too, whooping in joy.

But Megan being Megan, she ran inside her dorm and grabbed her own towel! Megan grinned evilly and started to zipline too! Though... this was all part of the plan. Lilly knew Megan well enough to predict that she would try and copy them.

"Do your thing, Lilly!" grinned Lucy, handing the scissors to her friend.

Lilly smirked and snatched the scissors. She went to the rope and positioned the scissors. *Snip snip snip.*

You all know what that meant...

...Lilly had cut the rope! Therefore, Megan tumbled noisily into the freezing sea, trying to swim out. This was their plan!

"Ha!" laughed the girls.

"AAH!" yelped Megan.

They had done it! Megan was now icy and wet, shouting in shock. Lilly laughed and laughed, dropping her towel onto the floor. Mia laughed the most. Being the naughtiest of her friends, Mia couldn't help but chuckle for ages.

Once they had gotten over the funny prank, Lilly reached for the box. It was beautiful! It was lustrous and radiant, with pearls on each side. Mermaid carvings were on the top of the box, bright like stars. A picture of the Crystal Clam was on the front, and the mermaid Lilly had seen in her dream was at the back of it.

Lilly forced the lid open. A bright light dazzled her eyes. She peered inside and saw a letter... and the Crystal Clam itself!

Dear girls,

I am extremely grateful! I thank you for all your hard work, you've found the Crystal Clam!

Tonight, you must come to Mermaid Lagoon! Remember, say: "I AM A MERMAID!" Did you ever wonder why there are only 4 words to say? Well, there are 4 of you! How else? But you must say it in the sea, or it doesn't work! And remember, bring the Crystal Clam.

Thank you, Queen Maia.

P.S: The spy will always be behind you. I MEAN it!

"We did it!" whooped Mia.

"And we can go to the Lagoon!" shouted Chloe.

"We're heroes!" yelled Lucy.

But Lilly felt something at the bottom of her heart. Queen Maia's words sounded urgent on the P.S part of the letter. *The spy will always be behind you,* Lilly recalled. Wait a minute... Oh no!

Lilly realized what the Queen had meant.

It was obvious now.

The truth dawned on her...

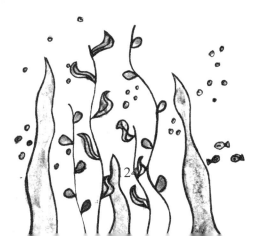

Chapter Eight

Dead

"I know you're there, Megan!" hissed Lilly, turning around.

Megan was JUST THERE! Behind her! That was what Queen Maia was trying to tell them! Megan stood in the doorway, soaking wet. Lilly almost felt like laughing, because several strands of seaweed balanced precariously on Megan's head.

"Oh, Lilly, Lilly. I knew I had to watch out for you," smirked Megan slyly.

"How in the world did you even get in here?" asked Chloe.

"Get in? The better question is, how do we get her out?" sighed Mia.

"We just won! Now she's back!" groaned Lucy.

"Now, give me the box!" yelled Megan.

"OK," laughed Mia.

"What? Mia! No!" screamed the girls frantically. But Mia just put the Crystal Clam on her bed and tossed the box to Megan.

"There, all yours!" chuckled Mia, laughing so much that she had to sit down.

"I want the CLAM! This is no time for jokes! You'll be sorry!" scowled Megan, chucking the box on the floor.

She clicked her fingers and a tiger appeared in there front of them. It did not growl, it just bared its teeth alarmingly. "Help!" squealed Mia, Chloe and Lucy.

"No! I know what you're doing," realized Lilly.

"What?" gasped Megan.

Lilly just laughed at the tiger and stuck her hand out towards the animal.

Her hand went straight through the tiger, as if it was a ghost!

"It's not real. All of these things are illusions!" grinned Lilly.

"How?" asked Mia.

Lilly grinned even more.

"I have proof! *One*, the gorilla. When we were trying to get the moon/cake, the gorilla swam towards us! Gorillas can't swim! *Two*, the ogre. Megan created an ogre to scare Chloe whilst surfing. But the ogre was *hovering!* It was in the air. And everyone knows that ogres don't fly. *Three*, the tiger. Megan just created a tiger out of thin air. The tiger's angry, but when tigers are angry, they display twisted ears. My brother Zack told me that, and the tiger here isn't doing that at all! Besides, I can just stick my hand through the tiger! Didn't you just see that?"

Megan seemed beaten. She was an angry shade of red, and her fists were clenched, ready to fight.

"Your powers can't harm us, we know the truth," continued Lilly. "This power is only dangerous to those who haven't worked it out yet."

Megan just stood still. But then she lunged forward and snatched the Crystal Clam!

"That's ours!" shrieked the girls, running after her.

Megan practically flew out the door, running like the wind. She tore along the pier and skidded around the dorms. It was a wonder that she didn't fall over.

Lilly and her friends dashed towards her, furious. Lilly now had a bleeding foot from tripping over a sharp stone.

Anger in her eyes.

But determination in her mind.

The mermaids had to be saved.

So she had to give it all she had.

No matter what.

She felt like a rocket that was lurching into space, and that determination let her go even faster. She ran and ran and ran, and was now even further ahead of Chloe!

Just after a mere 30 seconds, Lilly had caught up to Megan. Megan was not very fast, probably because she had lived underwater, in the Shadow Realm, meaning she was much better at swimming.

"Give us the clam!" roared Lilly.

"No!" howled Megan.

"Why do you need it anyway? Why do you want it? Why can't we have it back?" shrieked Lilly.

"She wants to make sure that Mermaid Lagoon isn't safe, why else?" whispered Lucy.

Lilly then leapt forwards and tried to grab the Crystal Clam from Megan. She seized it, but Megan still had a hold of it.

"Mine!" shouted Lilly.

"Mine!" shouted Megan.

Lilly pulled.

Megan pulled.

"Ooh, tug of war! Let's watch!" screamed Mia.

"For goodness sake, it's not a game!" screamed Chloe.

Megan dramatically pulled her fist back, fuming with anger. If Megan was a volcano, she'd probably erupt. Pushing her fist forwards, she struck Lilly's head. Lilly tumbled to the ground, dropping the clam.

SMASH!

What happened? I hear you ask. Well, something dreadful. All that was left of the Crystal Clam was... pieces. It was broken.

"NO! I can't stay like this!" sobbed Megan.

The other girls were too worried about Lilly to concentrate on the Crystal Clam or Megan's words.

Lilly opened her eyes. She sat up and stared. She saw white. She heard nothing. *She... wait, was she dead?*

"Oh no, am I dead? I can't be. I can't! I need to go back!" gasped Lilly. But Lilly heard a voice. She couldn't figure out who it was. Though that wasn't important. Lilly only needed to focus on the person's words.

"You have come a long way, Lilly," whispered the voice.

"Yes, yes, yes, I know. Wait... I've come a long way? Is that a good thing? Though never mind. I just want to know where I am," Lilly pleaded.

"Just dead," replied the voice.

"DEAD? No, no, no, please be kidding!" screamed Lilly.

"First you say 'yes, yes, yes.' Then you say 'no, no, no.' And I am not kidding. You are dead," repeated the voice.

"NO! NO! NO!" yelled Lilly.

This was bad. Really bad. EXTREMELY BAD! Lilly felt lost. Just lost. She had her chance to help Mermaid Lagoon. Why, oh why did she not duck when Megan tried to hit her?

"Enough shouting. You will be brought back to life," the voice told her.

"Huh? I can live?" puffed Lilly.

"Yes. The world needs you. Just remember, trust. That is all you need," reminded the voice. "Trust. Trust. Trust..."

Lilly looked up. Her head was throbbing with pain, but she sat up and rubbed her eyes. She was alive!

"I'M NOT DEAD! YAY!" screeched Lilly.

"You're not dead. What made you think that?" asked Mia.

"I was. I WAS dead," said Lilly, and explained it all.

"Let's get Megan!" screamed Chloe.

"Yes!" agreed Lucy.

"Goodbye, spy!" shouted Mia.

The girls raised their fists. But Lilly stopped. She stopped.

Yes, I mean it!

Lilly recalled the words of that voice when she was dead. *Trust.* That was all she needed.

"I trust you, Megan. And I think there's more to your story," said Lilly.

"WHAT? No, no, Lilly, why are you trusting her?" shrieked Mia, suddenly acting sensible.

"Megan's evil! Stop!" roared Chloe, jumping up and down.

"She killed you! Don't trust her!" yelled Lucy, glaring at Megan.

Megan did not try to hurt anyone. She sighed and then slowly sat down. She picked up what was left of the Crystal Clam. This was the moment she told her story...

"Once, in those happy days, I was a mermaid-"

"GASP!" exclaimed Mia. Everyone turned to look at her. "Oh, wait, nothing exciting is happening yet. Wrong timing. Sorry. Carry on."

Megan rolled her eyes. "Sometimes the Shadow Realm would attack and take mermaids. I was one of those who were taken. Mermaid Lagoon had no idea of what happened to the stolen mermaids. Well, they got turned into evil spirits, and would be forced to fight Mermaid Lagoon. It's not a nice experience. They sent me to find the Crystal Clam once it got lost in the human world. It's quite peculiar in this world, you know.

Such different foods. Funny beds. And legs. No tails. And I want to get the Crystal Clam, because the Shadow Realm promised to turn me into a mermaid once I give it to them!"

The girls saw it all. Megan was just trying to get back to Mermaid Lagoon! She had been a mermaid, and that was why she had such an enormous passion for the sea. Lilly saw the truth in Megan's eyes. What Megan had just said was real.

"We didn't know that," said Lilly.

"Exactly. And now the clam's broken," said Megan.

"Can we fix it?" said Chloe.

"Only the golden pearl from the Crystal Clam can do that. But I don't have the pearl," said Megan.

"I do!" said Lilly.

Lilly offered the pearl and held it towards what was left of the Crystal Clam. The pearl span round and round, glowing golden. The Crystal Clam pieces started to lift and join together, and the pearl was gently sucked inside. Lilly inspected the clam. It was mended. It was as if it had never been broken.

"The pearl keeps it from breaking. That's why it didn't break when a spirit tried to cut it in half," said Megan.

"It's fixed, now what do we do?" said Lucy.

"We find Queen Maia. She will definitely change Megan back into a mermaid. If we try and go to the Shadow Realm, Megan will be a mermaid again, but then she'll just be a prisoner!" said Lilly.

"Are you sure? If I go to Mermaid Lagoon, I'll be in my spirit form, so I won't look like a human or a mermaid," said Megan.

"That's fine. We'll explain it all," said Lilly.

The girls went to the edge of the pier, and hopped into the water. Lilly shivered. The sea was all bitter in the evening, and her bleeding foot stung like mad.

"I AM A MERMAID!" they all screeched.

Thirty seconds passed. Nothing.

A minute passed. Still nothing.

Several minutes passed. Nothing- hey, wait, don't be impatient. This time, something did happen.

A strong current suddenly pulled the girls out to sea. They started to swirl round and round, and it made Lilly want to faint.

"Oh no!" groaned Lilly. "This is a whirlpool! I read about these in a book!"

Remember that book? It was the one Zack gave to her. And now there was really one! How unfortunate for them!

It went round and round and round...

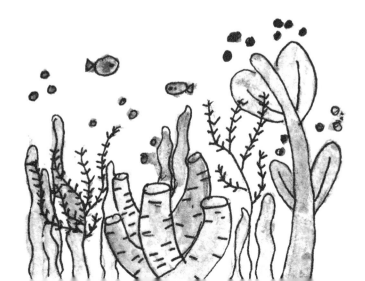

Chapter Nine

WAR!

BANG! CRASH! THUMP! "OW!"

Lilly had landed in the sea! She tried to get up, but it wasn't working.

"Oh no! Did I die *again?*" screamed Lilly.

"Ha! Of course you didn't die!" laughed Megan. "You don't walk, you swim!"

Lilly saw a glistening pink tail attached to her body! She had become a mermaid! She had even longer hair than usual, and she saw a starfish placed beautifully in her hair. All her friends looked great too, but it wasn't the same for Megan.

Megan was a mermaid too, but she was different. She resembled a grey cloud in the shape of a mermaid, only with red piercing eyes. She noticed Lilly staring and sighed.

"Yeah, I know. Evil spirits look like this. Ugly," said Megan, folding her arms.

"It's not that bad," said Lilly, though it was an obvious lie.

She then gazed at the waters. It was a dull grey, and it felt like someone (or some mermaid) was watching them. The fish seemed bored, and the sand was nowhere near golden. Not a pretty sight.

"Oh, do stop talking!" said Mia. "We've got to get this clam to the Queen!"

"Then where is the Queen?" asked Chloe.

"Hello, who are you?" said a fish. The fish was silvery-grey and wore a small top hat.

"We are here to save Mermaid Lagoon. But how can you talk? Fish don't talk, and the other fish won't talk either," said Lilly.

"Fever? Oh no, you must be sick!" said the fish.

"Ha! Lilly's not sick at all! Except for her foot that's bleeding- oh wait, we have tails now!" giggled Mia.

"But I didn't say that," said Lilly.

"Cat? I'm terribly sorry, but there are no cats in the sea," said the fish.

"Unless you count the cat on Chloe's t-shirt!" chuckled Mia.

"I didn't say cat, and I already know there are no cats in the sea. Cats hate water anyway," said Lilly.

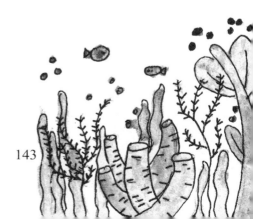

"Play? Well, this isn't the best time to play, but OK. What do you want to play?" said the fish.

"Hmm, maybe he's deaf," thought Mia.

"I am NOT deaf!" he yelled, suddenly hearing perfectly.

The girls covered their ears. The fish was louder than expected. Unfortunately, the fish's ear-piercing yells summoned an unwelcome guest. A tall, dark shadow loomed over them.

"Who are you?" boomed the shadow's voice. "Megan! Why are you with those mermaids?"

"He's the Shadow King," whimpered Megan.

The Shadow King was like a bigger version of Megan. He had a long staff with a crystal inside of it, and a dark crown sat on his head. His eyes were a darker red than anyone's, and his eyes were staring right at them!

"I-I-I just wanted to, um, err..." stammered Megan.

"YOU HAVE BETRAYED US!" he shouted.

Lilly trembled in fear, even though the Shadow King wasn't talking to her. His voice was loud like a lion's roar, and Megan just stared at the ground.

"Let's run!" said Lilly. "Wait, I mean swim!"

Swimming was not as easy as running. (Well, for Lilly it was like that.) But Megan was way ahead of them, trying to hide.

This made the Shadow King angry.

He pointed his staff towards them and dark bolts of lightning whizzed towards them. *Huh? I thought lightning couldn't travel underwater,* thought Lilly.

A sleek dolphin suddenly whizzed past. He seemed friendly and had blue shining eyes, not at all like the fish Lilly had met previously. Lilly was also surprised by his speed.

"I'm Bubbles, Queen Maia's pet dolphin. Quick, into that alley!" he hissed, swimming into a passage.

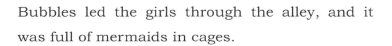

Lilly was also puzzled at how he could talk, but there was no time to ask. Any minute the Shadow King would find them.

Bubbles led the girls through the alley, and it was full of mermaids in cages.

Their eyes lit up as they saw them, but shivered as they saw Megan. At the end of the alley, there was one last cage with another mermaid trapped inside. A mermaid with an orange tail. A mermaid with a shiny crown. A mermaid called... *Queen Maia!*

"Hello, Your Majesty," said the girls, bowing.

They were bowing because how could you curtsy with a tail?

"Well done, girls. I have waited long for your arrival. And may I ask, why are those spirits with you?" said the Queen.

"Megan used to be a mermaid," said Lilly, and recounted the whole story to her. Queen Maia nodded and promised to change Megan back into a mermaid.

"Also, did *you* tell me to trust Megan when I was dead?" said Lilly.

"No, it wasn't me. Though I think I know who it could have been, my mother, Gina.

She is no longer here, but she was Queen of the Lagoon, before me. She only speaks to those who are truly special. She hasn't even spoken to me," said Queen Maia. "That means you are special, Lilly. Very special indeed."

"Erm, sorry to interrupt you, Your Majesty, but why did you say 'those spirits'?" asked Megan.

"Look behind you," said Queen Maia.

All of the girls turned around. A whole army of spirits were behind them! They frowned at them, and their swords were clutched.

"Uh oh!" said Mia.

"What do we do?" asked Chloe.

"We run- I mean, *swim* away?" said Lucy.

But there was no escape. A whole other army of spirits were on the other side of the alley! Lilly took a deep breath and tried to calm down. If she was on her own, she'd scream and scream and scream.

"We fight!" said Megan.

That was a ridiculous idea, of course.

They had no weapons at all, and the people of the Shadow Realm were armed with countless petrifying things, prepared for battle with, including:

* Daggers	* Bow and arrows
* Swords	* Throwing stars
* Maces	* Crossbows
* Cannons	* Spiked chains
* Catapults	* Bombs
* Slingshots	* Guns
* Axes	* _____

Gosh, that's a lot of weapons! Though the last space is blank. The blank space is for you to fill in whatever weapon you like. The Shadow Realm surely has it.

"POWERS!" yelled Lilly.

At once, Mia, Chloe and Lucy knew what to do. They jumped up and began to fight with their magic.

Soon there was a whole flurry of heat, ice and bubbles. Lilly was secretly glad that she didn't have her powers yet, because she didn't want to battle anyone.

"Why aren't you helping?" asked Queen Maia.

"I don't have my powers yet," replied Lilly.

"Where's the book I gave you?" questioned the Queen.

"It's back in my world- well, for you it's the *Terrifying Land Of Humans*," sighed Lilly.

"There's too many of them!" yelled Mia.

"They keep on coming, we can't do this all day!" cried Chloe.

"And we're tired," moaned Lucy.

Lilly was frozen to the spot. After all their hard work, now they would suddenly lose. Mermaid Lagoon would be like this forever.

"I know what to do," said the Queen. "We can sacrifice this."

She put her hand in Lilly's. Wait... What did this mean?

"We... sacrifice you?" said Lilly. "But then there won't be a queen!"

This was madness. *Someone* might have had to be sacrificed- but of all mermaids, why did it have to be the Queen?

Despite all of the pain that the mermaids had been through, the Queen was determined to save the Lagoon. And that meant that she had to sacrifice herself.

"A new mermaid will rule," said the Queen.

"OK then, but how do we even sacrifice something? And if we even manage to do that, what will even happen?" said Megan. "I did learn a lot about magic in the Shadow Realm, but I honestly have no idea how to sacrifice something."

"You will see," said the Queen. "First we must get all of you to combine your powers. Sorry Megan, you won't be able to help, because you're an evil spirit at the moment."

"But I don't have any," said Lilly.

The Queen handed over a book. It was the same one! The same one that Lilly had, and now her power could be revealed!

- Confident mermaids have ocean current powers
- Sporty mermaids have bubble powers
- Shy mermaids have whirlpool powers

Lilly then went to read about whirlpool powers. Hooray! She had found out her power! Even though she was the last to find her magic, she felt very proud indeed. But now she had to find out how to activate it.

1. Put your hands together and turn them around slowly, as if there is a ball in your hands.

2. A ball of water will appear.

3. Squeeze the ball as if you are moulding clay. Squeeze it into a whirlpool shape.

4. Push the whirlpool to where you want it to go.

Note: This power is very much like bubble powers, meaning the longer you squeeze it, the bigger the whirlpool.

"Ready?" asked Queen Maia.

"Ready!" replied everyone.

They each made a strong torrent of whatever power they had, and aimed it at Queen Maia. Lilly sighed a little. She had just met the Queen. Now she was going to go.

But when Lilly tried to make her whirlpool, it didn't work! She tried again. And again. And again. Still nothing happened! Why?

Straining with effort, nothing happened. It was quite mysterious, but also annoying.

"It's not working!" moaned Lilly.

"Maybe your personality isn't shy," said Mia.

"Huh? I thought I was shy," said Lilly.

"You *used* to be shy, but not anymore," said Chloe.

"Yeah, you died and came back! You're brave," said Lucy.

Lilly read more of the book. Her eyes were drawn to one sentence:

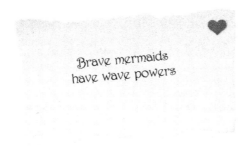

Brave mermaids
have wave powers

So maybe she had *wave* powers! The Queen looked impressed.

"Wave powers are hard to control. But you are special, like I said, Lilly. You can do it," urged the queen.

1. Spin around.
2. Whilst you are doing that, pull your hands together.
3. Push your hands away from you.
4. You will summon a wave.

Note: This power is one of the hardest ones to control. But once mastered, they can be very powerful and handy. The longer you spin, the bigger the wave.

Lilly then aimed a small-ish wave at Queen Maia.

(It was small-ish because waves are usually big, and Lilly had never seen a tiny one.)

"Thank you for your acquaintance. I hope we will meet again someday. And work together!" reminded the Queen, and with that, the Queen suddenly disappeared! In her place sat a sword! The sword had carved pictures on it from their adventure, and it looked as if it was made of crystal.

"We have a sword. What do we even do with it?" said Chloe.

"We use it to kill all those   spirits, what else?" said Mia.

"Well, how do you even use a sword?" said Lucy.

"Good point. I can't even pick it up," said Megan.

Lilly and her friends peered at the sword. Hmm. How could they use it if it was too heavy? "Work together. Work together," Lilly muttered to herself. That was what the Queen had said.

"I know!" said Lilly. "We work together!" And with that said, the sword glowed. It shone like stars and then multiplied into lots of swords! Lilly tried to pick one up. It worked!

"Now we each have one," said Lilly. "Come on! WAR!"

They speedily unlocked the other mermaid's cages and made sure to give them swords too. It was time to finish what the Shadow Realm started!

Lilly found herself being brave. Being bold, like nothing she had ever felt before. She was acting as if she was fearless! And she found that she was! On this incredible journey, she had eaten a wet cake, climbed a beanstalk, gone surfing, and even died and made it back to life! It had been a *true adventure.*

But the story isn't finished! So stay and
don't shut this book! They still had to
battle. And oh dear, it wasn't the best
experience! The sky (or water, in this case)
began to darken. Animals of all kinds started
to panic and swim away. Mermaids were
injured, and Lilly ended up with a gash on
her forehead. Despite this, courage made her
get up. She was going to save Mermaid
Lagoon!

With a loud yell and a strong heart, Lilly leapt up towards the surface. As she fell down to the seabed, she struck her sword into the ground.

BOOM!

A whole blast of light zoomed across the Lagoon. The whole place instantly lit up, and the people of the Shadow Realm (except Megan) were blinded by the light. They vanished. Mermaid Lagoon had won.

The citizens cheered loudly. Mermaid Lagoon

was safe. The war had ended! Mermaid Lagoon had won! All thanks to Lilly and her friends! Everyone cheered, but no-one louder than Lilly. It had been an amazing journey.

"You have helped our kingdom thrive once more," beamed Bubbles the dolphin. "Is there anything you wish to have, in return for your service?"

"There's one thing I want," said Lilly. "I want to be someone brave. Someone who fights for justice. Someone who always helps others. But I think I already have that."

"And that is true!" said Bubbles. "You and your friends will forever be remembered in the history of the Lagoon."

Lilly turned to Megan. "Thanks for your help," she said.

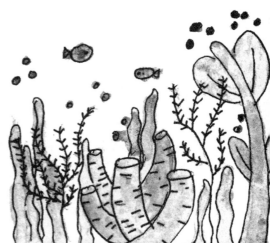

But Megan was not a shadow anymore. She had become a beautiful mermaid, with a bright tail and long black hair. Sitting upon her head, now sat a shining crown.

"Hmm. This crown wasn't here before," said Megan.

"I know! You're the new queen! Wait, Queen or Princess? What's the difference?" asked Lilly.

"Not sure," said Mia.

"Me neither," said Chloe.

"Same," echoed Lucy.

"Oh well, Princess Megan sounds better," declared Lilly. "All hail Princess Megan!"

"All hail Princess Megan!" echoed everyone else.

Megan turned to them. "I can't thank you enough. Please come back one day. What can I do for you in return?"

"I know!" shouted Mia. "Just don't be evil!"

"Ha!" laughed Megan. "As if I'd do that again! Anyways, OK!"

"You're welcome. You can now visit us in dreams, just like Queen Maia did. Are you going to stay here, at the Lagoon?" asked Lilly.

"Yes. Mermaid Lagoon is my true home," smiled Megan.

"But how do we get back? Do we have to swim?" queried Lilly.

With those words, Megan summoned a small current of water (possibly through her mermaid power) that brought them back to Ocean Academy.

Chapter Ten

The Book

"Good morning!" Lilly had just woken up. It had been a tiring few days after the war, and she had a spring in her step. Today was the day that Miss Jannah was going to announce the dorm winner! If they won, they would get a free next term!

She skipped outside and beamed like the sun. She went near the pier and whispered, "Hello Megan. Today is the day to find out who wins the next free term!"

Lilly knew Megan would never come up to the surface to chat, because she wouldn't want anyone to see her as a mermaid. But something told Lilly that Megan could hear her.

When it was time to announce the winning dorm, Lilly held her breath.

If Emerald dorm won, she could come and visit Mermaid Lagoon with her friends once more.

"Thank you all for taking part in this competition. Here are the results!" said Miss Jannah. "Ruby dorm with 560 points. Diamond dorm with 632 points. Sapphire dorm with 843 points. So the winning dorm is... Emerald dorm, with an amazing number of 1,000 points!"

All of those in Emerald dorm leapt up in the air. They had won! It meant their next term would be free! Lilly could not believe what she had just heard. She was a winner!

That wasn't the only surprise that had happened! In the afternoon, Lilly spotted a letter made out of seaweed on her bed. Though it had left a salty puddle of water on her duvet. She wondered how to clean it up before anyone saw it.

But she was focused on the letter.

Who was it from?

Dear Lilly, Mia, Chloe and Lucy,

Princess Megan here! (But it's just Megan to you.) You have been invited to a party in Mermaid Lagoon to celebrate the success of the Crystal Clam! (But about Queen Maia, I wish she was alive.)

Your story to return the Crystal Clam has been spread all over the Lagoon! You are all heroes.

You do not need to come to Mermaid Lagoon!

I will take you in your dreams! It will be a dream, but real!

See you tonight,

Princess Megan.

P.S There will be a lot of mermaids who will probably want signatures. Do keep that in mind!

The girls were extremely excited! They bounced up and down happily and began to chat.

"Oooh, I can't wait to try the food!" said Lucy.

"I wonder if we'll play some games!" said Mia.

"Will we be given gifts?" said Chloe.

Lilly didn't mind what happened, she just wanted to go! (Unless there was a whirlpool, of course...)

Once the sun began to set, Lilly shut her eyes. She really wanted to go to the party, but that meant she had to sleep first. If not, she'd miss it! She took a deep breath and pulled the blanket over her head.

"Hooray!" cheered a sudden voice. It was Megan. "You're here at last!"

Lilly looked down and saw the pink gleam of her elegant tail. She was at the party! She saw her friends beside her, grinning like mad.

"Wow. Are we actually here, since this is a dream?" asked Lilly.

"Yes. It is a dream but it is all real. All queen mermaids have this sort of power. It's very useful!" said Megan proudly.

Lilly peered over her shoulder. She stared at a table made of shells, and a dark purple cloth lay over it. The table was laid with all sorts of foods!

"Oooh! What are these?" said Lilly, curious.

There were new sorts of food, and they tasted quite nice! There were cakes that were small and very fluffy, as fluffy as pink candyfloss.

There were pots with a black sauce in them. The sauce was so black, that anyone could've mistaken it for a pot of ink.

Lilly tried some shiny round sweets that just burst in your mouth. They tasted a lot like spoonfuls of sugar... hopefully they weren't too unhealthy.

The mermaids surrounding her were all drinking out of shells, so Lilly tried her best to follow their etiquette.

"What are these cakes? And what are the sweets made out of? Oh, and I like this sauce! But why is it black and cloudy?" Lilly questioned rapidly.

She had a habit of asking too many questions at once, as you may have noticed throughout this book.

"The cakes, whatever cakes are, they're sea sponges, a traditional recipe. The sweets are called Whirl-Pearls, and they're made out of pearls. Duh! And that sauce is black because it's squid ink," explained a mermaid with a long ponytail that reached her hips.

"Whaaat?" said Lilly.

She looked at the food in both wonder and disgust. Was the food really what the mermaid had told her?

Hmm. She then stared at Lucy, who was writing down some recipes of the food.

(Though somehow the paper didn't dissolve! How

strange.) Lucy didn't seem to mind at all.

Lilly then tugged at her clothes. She had always thought that mermaids wore shells on their chests.

"How can mermaids wear shirts under the sea? How do they get the material?" asked Lilly.

"We make them out of kelp," replied the same mermaid.

"Eww! Wait, but my clothes aren't green. And kelp is green," thought Lilly.

"That's correct. We dunk the clothes in coloured-squid ink. Then we get all sorts of coloured clothing. Humans are so silly. They think we just wear shells all day.

Shells are uncomfortable, you know! If that was true, what about boy mermaids? Imagine them wearing shells!

Even worse!" explained the mermaid, laughing at the thought.

"More squid ink? Argh!" yelled Lilly, pushing her pot of sauce away from her. "Hold on... I have one more question."

"Yes?" the mermaid responded, rolling her eyes. She seemed very tired of Lilly's questions.

"You're wearing a shirt with a picture of a human on it. Why? You're a mermaid," questioned Lilly.

"Don't humans have shirts with pictures of mermaids on them?" grinned the mermaid.

"I suppose so," muttered Lilly, thinking of her t-shirt that had a mermaid on it.

"See! Anyways, is that the last of your questions?" queried the mermaid.

"Yes, that's enough questions," smiled Lilly. The mermaid dashed away, not wanting to answer anything else!

"WAIT! One more question!" shouted Lilly. But the mermaid had already disappeared.

Megan came over, just as Lilly was saying, "That silly mermaid! She can't expect me to know anything about mermaids and yet she turns her nose up at me as if I am the silliest person on earth!"

"Lilly..." said Megan. "That's my sister..."

"WHAT?" said Lilly. "Um, err... I was kidding!"

"Ha! Ha!" giggled Megan. "I don't even have a sister! You fell for that so easily!"

Lilly couldn't help but laugh too. Naughty Megan, tricking Lilly like that!

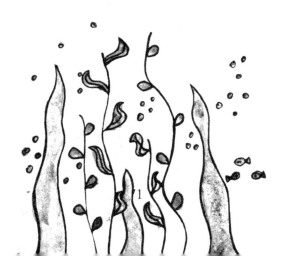

Then a sudden BANG caused all of the mermaids to cheer. (But not Lilly.) She then saw a whopping fireworks display! Fireworks don't work underwater, so instead they were shells with a special sort of powder in them. The fireworks flew up into the air and exploded into stars and trails of dust. The fireworks' dust trails flew into the shapes of Lilly and her friends!

Afterwards, Lilly and her friends were each presented an identical gift. They were some necklaces that were made out of pearls.

"These pearls will let you talk to each other. Just tap them and say the name of the friend you would like to talk to," said Megan.

"This is amazing. Thank you so much. We also won the dorm competition, so we'll definitely come back and visit next term!" said Lilly.

"I'll wake you up now. Bye!" said Megan.

"Bye!" said the girls.

Lilly blinked. She looked up and saw that she was in Emerald dorm. She was back! But something in her heart felt wrong.

I have to go back home today, thought Lilly. It was the end of term. So unfortunately, yes. She had to go home.

"I'll miss you all," said Lilly.

"Yeah. But we have these pearls so that we can talk to each other," said Mia.

"Yep. That'll be great!" said Chloe.

"Next term we'll come back here, and visit all the mermaids again," said Lucy.

"Yes, we will!" said Lilly.

It was a long trip back. This time, Lilly kept track of the time and made sure that they didn't have to parachute!

Although she had to say goodbye to her friends, Lilly knew that they would meet again someday.

Once she was home, Lilly was greeted by her family. She was extremely happy to see them, and settled down on her bed. But a thought struck her.

She began using her mum's computer to type a story. Lilly had thought, *I love to read. Let me type a story!*

You may be wondering what a story has to do with this book. But be patient.
You will find out.

Each day Lilly would spend about half an hour (or more!) typing.

Click, clack, click, clack, went the keyboard.

One afternoon, after about a month, Lilly had finished her story! She also had a friendly teacher who was helping to edit and improve her story and after a while, Lilly had her story published!

What did you say?

Repeat that question please!

Did you say that you wanted to read Lilly's story? Well, you are!

This is Lilly's story, right here in your hands!

And you've just finished reading it.

THE END

Moist Vanilla Cupcake Recipe

Hello reader,
this is Lilly here, and Lucy is also here to help
me with the recipe, since she's good at cooking.
Do you remember in this story, we made this
exact cake?
It makes about 15 cupcakes.

Ingredients

- 213g plain flour
- 110g caster sugar
- ¼tsp (1.25ml) baking soda
- 1½tsp (7.5ml) baking powder
- ¼tsp salt
- 170g unsalted butter (room temperature)
- 3 egg whites (room temperature)
- 1tbsp (15ml) vanilla extract
- 124ml Greek Style yoghurt
- 130ml whole milk (warm)

Instructions

1. Firstly, measure all of your ingredients.

2. Next, preheat the oven to 160°C.

3. Then, prepare your cupcake cases by sifting in the flour, caster sugar, salt, baking soda and baking powder in a large bowl. Whisk them together.

4. In another bowl, whisk the wet ingredients together. (The wet ingredients are: egg whites, vanilla extract, Greek Style yoghurt, milk, and butter.)
   (Also, you can just hand mix them, and don't worry about the clumpy butter.)

5. Afterwards, pour the wet ingredients into the dry ingredients. Mix them until they're combined.

6. Spoon out the batter into the cupcake cases.

7. Bake for about 25 minutes or until golden brown.

8. There's one last step...
   ENJOY!

Hello there, young reader.

This is Lilly!

Did you make the cupcakes?

If so, did you like them? Good!

I have tried making them on my own. They, erm, didn't turn out very well. First I forgot the sugar, and then my cakes were plain. Then I burnt my cakes and they tasted disgusting. After, I... Well, maybe I shouldn't mention that. In the end I asked Lucy to bake some instead and her cupcakes were PERFECT!

(This just proves how bad I am at cooking. Hey, it's not funny!)

Anyway, bye reader. I want to eat my- well, not mine- Lucy's- cupcakes. Bye!

About the Author

Thalia S. A. is a young author, who was born in Manchester, England.

She loved being read aloud to when she was a baby. She has developed a great passion for reading, apparently even chewing and eating her board books at around six months old.

Thalia's mum discovered that she could read at the age of three, when she was reading out loud, the title of Peppa Pig series on the television (perhaps too many words from the board books had been digested into her tummy, LOL).

Growing up in Warwickshire, Thalia is an avid reader and has won many drawing and writing competitions. She has been awarded by her school for consistently being a positive role model, extremely polite and a fabulous reader!

Some of her writings were published in anthologies alongside thousands of children from all over the United Kingdom by Young Writers.

Thalia S. A. enjoys doing voice overs with her cute little brother. She has been recording VO's for explainer videos, product ads, e-learning projects, narration and many more.

In addition, she likes art, cycling, playing squash, swimming and baking with her mum. She hates mathematics but is very grateful to have an engineer father who is a maths genius that makes her feel that maths is like magic!

Determined to aspire others through her books, Thalia inherits writing talents from her mother, who was once a young author (and also the partner illustrator for this particular book), her late grandfather Jamaludin D., who was a prolific poet and her grandmother Ramsiyah Amir who is an author. All of which come from Malaysia.

You can follow Thalia's creative journey on
Website: www.thaliasa.com
Facebook Page: Thalia S. A.
Instagram: misst_masterz

Printed in Great Britain
by Amazon

38051794R00106